More Perfect than the Moon

ALSO BY PATRICIA MACLACHLAN

PATRICIA MacLACHLAN

More Perfect than the Moon

JOANNA COTLER BOOKS
An Imprint of HarperCollins*Publishers*

Library of Congress Cataloging-in-Publication Data
MacLachlan, Patricia.
More perfect than the moon / Patricia MacLachlan.— 1st ed.
p. cm.
Sequel to: Caleb's story.
Summary: Eight-year-old Cassie Witting is upset when she finds
out that her mother, Sarah, is expecting a baby, but writing in the
journal that was her brother Caleb's helps her sort out her feelings
and she finally learns that Sarah will always love her.
ISBN 0-06-027558-8 — ISBN 0-06-027559-6 (lib. bdg.)
[1. Babies—Fiction. 2. Mothers and daughters—Fiction.
3. Frontier and pioneer life—Great Plains—Fiction. 4. Great
Plains—Fiction.] I. Title.
PZ7.M2225Mr 2004   2003022702
[Fic]—dc22
1 2 3 4 5 6 7 8 9 10

First Edition

For Joanna Cotler and Justin Chanda—
with appreciation
with love
—P.M.

More Perfect
than the Moon

Hello. I am writing here now. My brother Caleb says it is my turn to keep the journal. He is busy working the farm most of the time, and when haying time comes he'll be busy all the time.

I am almost in third grade. I can spell, you know. And I know many words, some of them important words. Like

windswept

imagination

ecstatic.

I will have to look up the meaning of ecstatic. But I can spell it.

I am a watcher. I am a listener, too. I am invisible. I can make myself so small and quiet and hidden that sometimes no one knows I am there to watch and listen.

Except for Grandfather. He finds me everywhere. He sees me when I'm hiding. Grandfather tells me he can see through walls.

But he won't stop me.
I will find lots to write about.
Watch me.
                    —Cassandra Sarah Witting

1

Summer was cool and wet, and the barn-yard was muddy. It was like spring left over. The cats jumped from the fence and ran into the barn so they could sleep in the dry hay.

"I see you there, you know," Grandfather called to me. "Hiding behind Martha."

Grandfather knew the names of all our cows. Martha was black, with a white spot on her rump.

I stood up.

"I'm not hiding," I said. "I'm studying Martha's spot."

This made Grandfather smile. And Caleb.

"You were hiding," said Grandfather. "It made Martha nervous. I could see her eyes roll."

Martha turned and stared at me.

"Martha always rolls her eyes," I told Grandfather.

He laughed out loud. He and Caleb were digging trenches in the mud so the rains would run off.

"You're sneaky, Cassie," said Caleb.

"Elusive," I told him. "Mama says I'm elusive."

"Sarah always finds a word to make you look better," said Caleb. "I say you're sneaky."

Caleb has always called Mama Sarah. My mama is not Caleb's real mama. But she is mine. He and Anna called her Sarah when she first came to meet Papa. Before they were married. I call her Mama. Maybe someday I'll call her Sarah.

"I'm looking for things to write about," I told Caleb. "It just looks like I'm sneaky."

The cows float into the dark barn and then out the other side into summer. It is hot and dusty. Heat waves rise off the land and the cows happily eat their way through the fields of corn. They walk into the cow pond and look up, and the birds flying across the sky swoop down to cool their faces with their wings.

And that's the truth.

I took my notebook out of my coat pocket and began reading to them.

"'Grandfather and Caleb dug deep rivers in the mud so the cows, Martha, Eleni, Princess, Mary Louise, Pudgie, and Boots, can float into the barn to feed.'"

"That's not the truth!" said Caleb.

"Yes it is," I said. "It is storytelling."

"Made up," said Caleb.

"Maybe," I said, turning away and walking through the mud to the barn. I turned once to see Grandfather smiling at me, Caleb staring.

"Maybe," I said louder just before I disappeared into the dark barn.

2

I saw many things. Mama had gained pounds this winter. Sometimes she wore Papa's sweaters.

"They seem to fit me better," she said. "And they smell like your papa."

Today in the barn I saw Papa put his arm around Grandfather. They laughed at something. I tiptoed in closer to hear what it was, but Grandfather, as always, saw me.

"Cassie? That you behind the stall?"

"Not a good thing, lurking, Cassie," said Papa with a frown.

"It would be a good thing if you didn't see me," I said crossly. "How am I ever going to find things to write about if I can't listen?"

"Maybe you need to observe, Cassie,"
said Papa. "Quietly. Without lurking."

I did observe. I saw more things.

I saw Caleb talking to a girl by the
pond. She rode a dappled horse.

"Who was that?" I asked.

"Someone," said Caleb. "Not for your
eyes."

Of course it was for my eyes.

---

*Caleb has found a princess. They meet
in secret because they must.*

*They will marry soon and run away
to live in wild Borneo, eating fruit and nuts
from the bushes there. They will have two
babies named Ondine and Tootie.*

I read Caleb my words to tease him. It worked.

"Wild Borneo!" said Caleb very loudly. "Not true, Cassie. And she is *not* a princess! How can you write such things?"

"Papa told me to observe quietly. That is what I saw," I said.

"It *is* a good story, though, Cassie," said Grandfather, smiling.

"Thank you."

"And Tootie is a very unusual name," said Papa.

"Imaginative," added Mama.

"Don't encourage her, Sarah," said Caleb. "Nothing she writes is the truth."

"It is *my* truth," I said. "Mine."

I saw more things. I saw that Mama took naps late morning and afternoon. I watched her from the side porch as she worked in her garden. She stopped working and put her hand to her throat as if she could be sick.

"In the morning she is the last to get

up," I whispered to Caleb and Grandfather in the kitchen. "She is always, always, always the first one up."

Caleb smiled at me.

"And how would you know that?" he asked. "We have to tumble you out of bed every morning."

Grandfather was slicing bread for lunch.

"Once I carried you all the way down the stairs wrapped in a blanket," he said. "I sat you at the breakfast table, and you were *still* asleep."

I frowned at Caleb and Grandfather, which made them smile all the more.

"You can tease if you want," I said. "But Mama's sick."

Grandfather and Caleb turned as Mama came into the house then, her hair in wisps around her face. She stopped when she saw us all watching her.

"This looks like a meeting," she said with a little smile.

Grandfather cleared his throat.

"No meeting. Lunch. What can I fix you, Sarah?"

Sarah shook her head and held up her hand.

"Nothing, thank you, John. No food."

"Are you ill, Sarah?" asked Grandfather.

Mama turned and smiled the smallest smile at Grandfather.

"I don't feel like eating. . . . I think I'll rest."

Papa came in the door.

"Sarah?" asked Papa.

"I'm going to lie down, Jacob."

Papa looked quickly at us, then followed Mama to the bedroom. I could hear his voice, soft, then hers.

No one spoke. Grandfather poured me a cup of milk.

"See? She is sick," I told him.

"Everyone gets sick, Cassie."

"Not Mama."

I could feel sudden tears at the corners of my eyes.

Caleb put his arm around me. I was surprised. Caleb never put his arm around me.

"Sarah will be fine, Cassie. You'll see."

I could tell that Caleb was worried, too, even though he didn't say so. Later I saw him watching Mama.

And that evening Mama didn't come to dinner. She stayed in her bed. Papa made biscuits that were hard and dry, like stones. Grandfather made a stew that needed salt. Caleb set the table with forks for the stew. No spoons. Even the dogs were restless. Nick and Lottie stood at Mama's bedroom door and looked at her. I watched her, too, until she turned her head and told us to go away.

"I'm fine, Cassie. Don't watch me. Go away and take the dogs," she said.

I didn't go away. I stood behind the door and kept watching her. After a long while I took the dogs up to bed with me.

Most nights Mama came up to kiss me good night. But no one came except for

Lottie and Nick. They lay on either side of me all through the night. They slept while I watched the moon move across the window and out over the barn. Across the meadow. Before I fell asleep the moon washed over the prairie, making it look soft and safe, covered by a silver quilt.

3

In the morning Lottie and Nick were gone, leaving dog dents in the quilt. I got out of bed quickly and dressed. I ran downstairs, stopping partway to listen. There were no sounds of talk in the kitchen. No sounds at all.

The table was set for breakfast. The coffeepot was on the stove. I touched it and pulled my hand away. Hot.

Very slowly I walked to the door of Mama and Papa's bedroom. Mama was asleep, the bedcovers tucked tightly around her. Lottie and Nick stood next to the bed, staring at her. They looked up at me as I came into the room. Nick wagged his tail.

We stood there for a long time, watching Mama breathe. Finally I took the dogs and went out through the kitchen to the yard. Papa was fixing a bridle. He smiled.

"You slept late."

I nodded.

"Your mama still sleeping?"

I nodded again.

"She needs rest, Cassie," said Papa.

"Why?" I asked.

Papa shook his head. He didn't answer my question why.

"She's going to see Dr. Sam."

I moved closer to Papa so he had to put his arm around me.

"May I go to town, too?"

"Not today, Cassie."

"I need to buy a new journal."

"Already? You've filled up that journal *already*? Didn't know there was that much going on here."

I smiled at Papa.

"There isn't. I make up things."

"What things?"

"Dreams. Wishes. What I want."

Papa grinned.

"That is a good way to fill it up. Maybe some of those things will come to be. One of the dreams. One of the wishes."

Papa kissed the top of my head. Out in the paddock Grandfather and Caleb cleaned and filled the cows' water tubs. Redwings flew in a wave over Caleb and Grandfather and the cows like a veil. A cloud passed by the sun and it was dark, then light again.

"Sarah. How are you feeling?" called Papa.

Mama walked out of the house. Grandfather and Caleb came to the fence.

Mama smiled. Slowly she walked toward us.

"Better," said Mama. "I missed dinner, didn't I? And breakfast."

Suddenly Mama stopped, putting up her hand to brush back her hair.

"Jacob?" Her voice sounded faraway.

"Sarah!" cried Papa.

He began to run toward her. Caleb jumped over the fence and ran, too, but it was Papa who caught Mama as she fainted.

———◆———

I stood so still. Papa carried Mama to the wagon.

"Caleb! Hitch up the horses. You'll drive to Dr. Sam's. Cassie, get a blanket!"

"I'll help," called Grandfather, touching me as he hurried by.

He turned and spoke harshly to me.

"Cassie! Blankets!"

His voice was strange. Stranger than I'd ever heard. I ran to the house, and the dogs began barking. I grabbed a blanket off Mama's bed and ran past Lottie and Nick.

"Hush!" I said to them.

I could feel tears coming down my face.

The horses were hitched up. Caleb climbed up to drive. Grandfather and Papa wrapped Mama in the blanket. Her face was as pale as summer clouds.

"Call Dr. Sam! Call Anna," said Papa as Caleb began to drive away. "Call now."

"Go. Go," said Grandfather.

He grabbed my hand and pulled me into the house with him as the wagon turned out of the yard and down the road.

He picked up the phone with one hand. With the other he gathered me close to him. I buried my face in his shirt and never heard him tell the operator to call Dr. Sam.

"Anna wants to talk to you, Cassie."

My sister's voice sounded faint and far-away.

"Cass? I know you're worried, but Sarah will be fine. Don't worry. Sam will take care of her."

I started to cry again.

"It's all right, Cassie," Grandfather said.

"No," I said, looking up into his face. It was as pale as Mama's.

"Maybe it is my fault. She told me not to watch her. I wish I hadn't watched her!"

I cried until Grandfather's shirt was wet with my tears.

———◆———

Grandfather and I fed the cows and the sheep while we waited. I tossed grain to the chickens, the chicks of Mama's chickens from long ago. I liked the sounds they made, happy and peaceful clucking, the same every day. Comforting. I remembered the first time I'd fed the chickens. I was so small, and when I was scared Papa lifted me up and up and up above the chickens and Mama laughed.

All of a sudden I remembered my papa's words: sometimes the hopes and dreams we write about may come to be. I tossed the last of the grain to the chickens and ran to get my journal. I lay on the daybed and wrote.

*Mama and Papa and Caleb drove to
town because Mama was sick. But she isn't
sick. She is well and happy and her cheeks
are rose colored again. When she comes
home, she brings me a small gift. A perfect
gift. More perfect than the moon.*

I laid my head on the pillow and read my
words. *A perfect gift. More perfect than the moon.* I
liked those words. They were good words.

I slept then. I dreamed about a perfect
gift.

———◆———

"Cassie. Cassie."

Grandfather was shaking my shoulder.

"You're dreaming, Cass. Wake up. Anna
wants to talk to you."

"Is Mama all right?"

"Sarah's fine."

I ran to the phone.

"Anna?" I could hardly catch my breath.

"Cassie, she's all right. She just left."

"She's coming home?!"

"Yes."

"Did Dr. Sam give her medicine?"

"She'll tell you, Cassie. When she gets there. I have to go now."

"Wait! Anna?"

"What?"

I took a deep breath.

"Is Mama bringing home a perfect gift?"

There was the sound of surprised silence on the phone line.

"Maybe," said Anna, her voice soft. "Maybe. Good-bye."

Before I could say good-bye back to Anna, she had hung up.

Grandfather took my hand and together we walked outside.

"Well now, I'd better get back to the chores," he said. He began to walk to the barn. He turned.

"Are you all right, Cassie?"

"Yes," I said. "I'm going to pick a bouquet of flowers for Mama."

"Perfect," said Grandfather, smiling.

Perfect.

More perfect than the moon.

4

"Cassie! They're coming!"

Grandfather's voice seemed to float from far away over the prairie grasses.

I stood in the fields with a handful of violets and yellow star grass and watched the wagon come up the road. Papa was driving, Mama sitting next to him.

Caleb waved from the back of the wagon. I waved back and began running through meadow grass and flowers. I jumped over the small stream that was filled with water, startling the cows. One of the sheep, Mattie, I think, began running beside me, and I could feel myself grinning. It felt strange to grin. I had been so sad and scared this morning.

The wagon stopped and Papa helped

Mama down. Caleb began to unhitch the horses.

"Your cheeks are rose colored!" I cried, making Papa smile. "You're not sick. It's just the way I wrote it!"

I handed Mama the flowers.

"Thank you, Cassie," Mama said.

"Let's get inside," said Papa.

Mama was silent. I looked sideways at her. Her lips were pressed together as if she didn't want to let words out.

"Aren't you happy that you're not sick?" I asked.

Mama took off her coat and sat down. She put my flowers on the kitchen table.

"I'll put these in water in a minute," she said.

Caleb came into the kitchen. Mama looked at him for the longest time.

"You're so tall, Caleb," she said softly. "I remember when I first came here. . . ." Her voice faded.

"I was little," said Caleb. "I was very little,

and Anna and I were very scared that you wouldn't stay. I wanted everything to be . . ." Caleb searched for the word.

"Perfect," I said quickly.

Everyone looked at me, and I could feel my face flush.

"You weren't born yet, Cassie," said Caleb softly.

"I know. But I read Anna's journals. Grandfather and I read them together."

"We did," said Grandfather.

"And you brought gifts from Maine for Anna and Caleb, Mama. A smooth sea stone and a shell."

"I did," said Mama.

One of the cats, Lily, brushed against my leg.

"And you brought Seal," I said. "All the way from Maine."

Mama leaned down to stroke Lily.

"Lily's grandmother," she said, her voice low.

"And then you became my mama," I said.

Mama looked at me then.

"What did you mean, Cassie? That I wasn't sick and that my cheeks were rose colored? And it was how you had written it?"

I got my journal.

"Papa said that wishes and hopes and dreams were good things to fill my journal. Maybe, he said, some of them would come true."

"He said that?"

I read her the part of what I had written:

"'When she comes home, she brings me a small gift. A perfect gift.

"'More perfect than the moon.'"

It was quiet in the room.

"I thought if I wrote you weren't sick then you would come home happy and well," I said.

"With a gift more perfect than the moon," whispered Sarah.

Papa leaned down to kiss Mama's cheek. And suddenly, surprising us all, Mama and

Papa both smiled. Not just smiles. They grinned.

"What's funny?" I asked.

Caleb smiled, too. Grandfather poured a cup of coffee and sat down at the kitchen table.

"Why are you smiling?" I asked Mama.

"Be patient, Cassie," said Grandfather. "I think they're about to tell us."

Now Mama's face was serious. So serious that I thought she might cry. I could see tears in her eyes.

"What you wrote, Cassie, is true. About a perfect gift," she said.

"It is?"

I moved over to Mama and she put an arm around me.

"What is the gift?" I asked.

"A baby," said Mama.

"Baby?" I asked.

Mama took a deep breath and looked at Caleb, then Grandfather, then me. She smiled at Papa.

"Our baby," she said. "We're going to have our baby."

There was a silence all around the room.

"*Our* baby," she repeated softly.

Our baby!

I moved away from Mama.

"I didn't want to tell you all earlier because . . ."

Mama stopped.

"Because she didn't want you to worry," said Papa. "She wanted everything to be all right."

When I spoke my voice did not sound like my voice.

"*Everything is not all right*," I said loudly. "And this is not *our* baby. It is *your* baby. Yours! And it is not the perfect gift! It isn't!"

"Cassie," said Grandfather, reaching out for my arm.

I pushed him away and ran out the door and through the yard. Lottie and Nick, sleeping on the porch, lifted their heads as I ran off. I ducked through the fence and ran across the meadow and to the fields and over the hill until I couldn't see the house anymore.

I sat behind the big tree on the hill, looking over the slough. The slough was filled with water from the summer rains. A family of ducks swam around the edges. Everything was peaceful and the way it had always been.

But things were not the same. Nothing would ever be the same. My throat hurt as if I might cry. I pulled out my journal and began writing to stop the tears from coming.

Mama and Papa should have brought me a new journal, but they didn't.

A baby is not a gift. Not the gift I wanted. A baby is a bother.

New glass marbles are gifts, blue and green and with cloudy swirls.

A new horse, a baby lamb are gifts.
Books are gifts, to read and read and
read again.
The new baby will be ugly and mean.
I will make it do all my chores.

There was a rustle beside me. Papa sat down. Lottie and Nick ran past us down to the water, sending up the ducks. I closed my journal.

"What are you writing about?" Papa asked.

"Gifts."

"I hope you put a new bridle in there," he said. "That's what I'm wanting."

Lottie and Nick waded into the water.

"Are you mad at me?" I asked.

"No. I'm not mad."

"Mama's mad, I bet."

"No. Mama's not mad, either."

"Why not?"

"She loves you," said Papa.

Lottie came out of the water and when she shook, the droplets caught the light.

"When you were born," said Papa very softly, "you were wondrous."

I had never heard Papa use that word before.

"Was I more perfect than the moon?"

"I don't think anything is perfect," he said. "Or anyone."

"Then why did you like me?"

"You smiled right off the bat."

"I don't think babies do that," I said.

"You did that. And you made small snuffling noises. And when I held you, you smelled like something sweet I'd never smelled before. Like spring roses."

That sounded perfect to me, but I didn't say so out loud.

"Did Anna and Caleb love me?"

"Yes. When you began to walk, you followed them around wherever they went."

"Did they hate that?"

"No. They thought you were funny."

"Well, I am not going to let the new baby follow me anywhere."

"That's up to you," said Papa.

Nick came out of the water then and started to walk up the hill to where we sat.

"I will not speak to the baby. And I will not look at the baby, either," I said.

"Watch out, Cassie," said Papa suddenly, taking my hand.

We stood up, but we were not fast enough. Nick shook water all over us. Papa and I laughed and ran back through the fields, dripping water, Lottie and Nick barking and leaping around us.

We jumped over the little brook and ran across the meadow to the house.

Mama's flowers were still on the kitchen table, dried and wilted. She had forgotten to put them in water.

I threw them away.

No matter what Papa says, I will not love the new baby.

5

Hot summer days came and the slough dried up. The hay had been cut once, but it was growing fast again. The dogs and I wound our way through the hay fields and through the corn. We made a nest in the shade of the corn. Lottie and Nick slept there as I wrote.

Summer is too hot. I can't write. I like winter. There is something sharp about winter that makes me think. I like writing all curled up in a corner of the warm house, safe and quiet. Out here in the open there is too much space. My thoughts fly away.

Mama is getting bigger every day. Soon she will float up and up and hover over us like a rain cloud.

"Cassie! Where are you?"

The dogs lifted their heads and thumped their tails. It was too hot to get up.

My sister Anna came through the corn, her face dusty.

"There you are."

She sat down next to me, reaching out to pet Lottie and Nick.

"You know, I used to hide out here, too."

I smiled.

"Grandfather says 'you know' all the time, too," I said.

"So do you. I remember when you didn't like Grandfather," said Anna.

"I was scared of him."

"Not anymore," said Anna.

"Grandfather knows everything," I said. "Sometimes *that's* scary."

Anna's long hair was the color of corn. She had caught it back in a blue ribbon.

"Why are you here?" I asked.

"Just came to visit. I brought some medicine for Grandfather. And to check on Sarah."

Anna lived in town now and worked for Dr. Sam. Once I had hidden behind the Russian olive bushes and had seen her kiss Justin, Dr. Sam's son. It was a long kiss and I had counted twenty-seven full seconds.

"And to see you, Cassie. And to tell you a secret."

"I'm tired of secrets," I said.

"You're never tired of secrets, Cass, you know."

Anna and I laughed at "you know."

"They told you about the baby?"

I nodded.

"It made me think about when you were born," Anna said.

"Papa said you loved me."

"Oh, not in the beginning, Cass."

I was surprised.

"But Papa said so."

"Well, I didn't tell Papa that I thought you were ugly and wrinkled and took too much of Sarah's time. I was about your age, Cass. I was very grown up and I didn't want any silly baby around."

I nodded.

"I will not look at or speak to this baby when it comes. I told Papa."

Anna didn't say anything.

I looked closely at her.

"What made you love me?"

Anna burst out laughing.

"I couldn't help it!" she said. "I just couldn't help it."

"Tell me," I said.

Anna shook her head, still laughing.

"I can't tell you why, Cass. You'll see."

No. I won't see.

The sun moved over us. Lottie and Nick crawled into the shade, panting. Anna and I lay back on the ground. There was a sweet smell of corn and earth all around us.

"What is the secret?" I asked.

Anna smiled.

"I knew you really weren't tired of secrets."

She held out her left hand for me to see. On her third finger was a gold ring, a sparkling stone in the middle.

"What does that mean?" I asked.

"It means Justin and I are getting married," said Anna. "No one else knows yet. I told you first."

I turned my head and smiled at her and she smiled back.

"I saw you kiss him for a lot of seconds once," I said.

"How many seconds?" asked Anna.

"Twenty-seven."

A cloud slipped over the sun and it was cool for a moment.

"Cass?"

"What?"

"I passed that record a long time ago."

Anna and I laughed. Someone called from the house and we went to tell Caleb and Grandfather and Mama and Papa that Anna was getting married and had kissed Justin for longer than twenty-seven seconds.

Anna and Justin got married and had eleven children, most of them girls. Mama gave birth to a baby lamb named Beatrice, and everyone lived happily ever after.

6

We drank lemonade under the big tree. The air was still. The dogs lay under the table. Mama fanned herself, her hair in wisps around her face.

"Someone's coming," said Grandfather.

We all turned to look at the cloud of dust rise up on the road. It was a horse and buggy.

"It's Matthew and Maggie," said Papa.

The buggy came into the yard and stopped.

Maggie climbed down from the wagon and put her arms around Mama.

"Sarah! You are big and lovely!" Maggie's voice was soft.

Mama smiled. Maggie had been Mama's very first friend when Mama came here from Maine. But when the drought came and there was no water, Matthew and Maggie and their children had moved away for two years. Mama and Maggie had written letters to each other every single day when Maggie had gone away.

And once I had seen Mama cry because she missed Maggie.

But now they were back.

Mama poured lemonade for Maggie and Matthew. She passed Matthew the homemade raisin cookies that he loved.

"I've missed these cookies, Sarah," said Matthew.

Mama smiled and brushed the hair back from her face.

"When's the day, Sarah?" asked Maggie.

"Soon. A few weeks . . . a month? The end of summer. The truth is I'm too old for this. This baby," said Mama. "I was too old when I came to live here."

I looked quickly at Mama. What did she mean "too old"?

"No. I'm old," said Papa.

"No, *I'm* old," said Grandfather, making everyone laugh.

"Grandfather wins," Caleb said.

Maggie put her arms around me.

"And Cassie, you are beautiful!"

No one had ever called me beautiful. They had called me sneaky and elusive and imaginative. Not beautiful.

"You look just like your mama."

I frowned. I looked at Mama. Big.

"I think I look like Anna," I said.

"Ah no," said Maggie. "You have your mama's smile and her eyes."

I frowned again.

"Actually, I think Cassie looks like Eleni, the cow," said Caleb.

There was laughter.

"No," said Mama. "*I* look like Eleni."

"Don't worry, Sarah. Eleni is a very beautiful cow," said Grandfather.

"I almost forgot, Cassie! Sarah asked me to get this for you," said Maggie. She handed me a small, flat, wrapped package. I took off the wrapping. It was a journal. I opened it. It was empty, no words.

I felt my throat tighten up. Mama hadn't forgotten after all.

"Thank you, Maggie," I said.

"It was your mama," said Maggie. "Thank her."

I looked at Mama.

"Thank you," I whispered.

Mama smiled. She reached out and took my hand.

"You need to keep writing, Cassie. You're a good writer."

My face felt hot. Mama hadn't seen what I'd written about her. She wouldn't like my writing if she read that.

I took the journal off behind the tree. I opened it. All of a sudden I felt far away. Far away from everyone. Far away from Mama.

I heard their talk about Anna and Justin getting married. I heard their talk about when Matthew would bring his horses for

the second haying. Talk of chores and gar-
dens and rain. Their words wound around
us like steam from hot tea.

---

*After Mama has the baby lamb,
Beatrice, she goes on long walks with me,
leaving Beatrice with Caleb.*

*"He can take care of her," she tells me.
"All she does is sleep and bleat.*

*"You are more beautiful than Beatrice,"
she tells me. "And you are much smarter.*

*"And Cassie, you are the finest writer
in the entire world.*

"I love you best."

I looked up, suddenly surprised at what I
had written. I closed the journal with a snap.

Something else was at the edges of my mind. Something that scared me. Something I had heard but couldn't remember. What was it?

———•◆•———

The house was dark and quiet when I sat straight up in bed. Lottie and Nick moved a little on the bed, but they didn't wake. Very slowly I got up. I looked out the window. There was a half-moon. I walked down the hallway to Caleb's bedroom. I pushed the door open.

Caleb slept in a tangle of blankets. I walked over quietly and sat on his bed. I waited. I didn't want to shake him. Sometimes Caleb was cross if you woke him. I waited, watching him for a long time. After a while he turned over. A book fell off the bed and hit the floor with a loud thump.

Caleb sat up, startled.

"What?"

"Shhh. A book fell off your bed," I said softly.

"What are you doing here, Cassie? Go away."

"I need to ask you something," I whispered.

"Not now. Tomorrow," mumbled Caleb.

"Please. Now, Caleb."

"What is it? What's wrong?" asked Caleb.

I took a deep breath.

"How old is Mama?"

"Oh Cassie. I don't know. Thirty-seven, thirty-eight. Go back to bed."

"Caleb? Why did Mama say she was too old?"

"I don't know. Go away."

"Caleb?"

"What?"

"How old was your mama when she had you? When she . . ."

I stopped. I couldn't say the word.

Caleb turned over, his back to me. He

didn't say anything. I got up and walked to the door. I walked back to my room and took out my journal. I couldn't say it but I could write it.

What if Mama is too old to have this baby? What if this terrible baby makes Mama die like Caleb's mama died when he was born?

I closed the journal as if shutting away the words would make them go away. But they didn't go away. I sat at the window watching for the longest time until the sun came up orange over the east meadow.

7

Mama was cooking pancakes in the big black skillet. The smell of melted butter and syrup filled the kitchen.

"You look tired, Cassie. Didn't you sleep well?" she asked me.

"No."

Mama put her hand on my forehead.

"You don't have a fever."

She handed me a cup of juice.

"Mama?"

"Yes?"

I didn't know how to ask her.

"Are you worried about being old?"

Mama burst out laughing. Then she stopped.

"You're serious, aren't you, Cass?"

Mama sat at the table.

"No, I don't worry about that. Why do you ask?"

"When Maggie was here, you said you were too old."

"I did say that, didn't I? I guess what I meant was that I'll have a new child to run after. Cassie, I thought I had the best life when I came here to be a mother to Anna and Caleb and marry your papa. And then I had you! And that seemed just perfect."

Perfect. That word again.

"But life has its ways, Cassie. This is something that I didn't expect."

"I didn't expect it, either," I said.

"No," said Mama softly. "You didn't."

Grandfather came in with Caleb then, and my talk with Mama was done. I still had the lump in my throat. I was still scared. I went out to feed the chickens. They didn't seem afraid of anything.

———•◆•———

Summer clouds rolled in, and Papa came out of the barn.

"Rain's coming," he said, squinting his eyes to see the faraway clouds.

"It was sunny just a bit ago," said Grandfather. "Summer storms come in fast."

"I hope it goes fast, too," said Papa. "We'll be haying soon."

The chickens didn't like rain, and when the first drops came they ran to the barn.

The geese had hatched goslings last week, and they had taken to following Mama everywhere. A large Mama getting larger. They followed her into the barn and out, down the road for walks, and today they tried to follow her into the house.

Caleb and I looked out the small barn window. The cows liked the rain and the coolness it brought. Eleni lifted her face to the rain, and when the wind came the horses ran out in the meadow.

"Was that you in my room?" asked Caleb. "In the night?"

"Yes."

"I thought maybe it was a dream."

I didn't say anything. Caleb looked down at me.

"It will be all right," he said. "I promise."

How could he promise that?

Thunder came then, drowning out anything I could say. I stood very still, looking out the barn window. After a while Caleb put his arm around me. We stood there for a long time as the rain pounded on the barn roof and chickens pecked around our feet.

———•◆•———

I watched day after day, but there wasn't much to write. Not much to make up. All I saw was the girl riding the dappled horse when she came again to see Caleb. It was Violet, Maggie and Matthew's daughter. They met behind the windmill. I heard them laughing and laughing there.

Princess Violet and Caleb are very happy. They laugh all day long. Their children, Ondine and Tootie, are growing up, and Tootie is getting a little fat even though she eats only nuts and fruits.

Caleb smiled when I read this to him. He was nicer to me now. He didn't seem to mind me writing stories about him. Sometimes he even liked them.

But writing was hard. Stories wouldn't come, and I said so to Grandfather. He nodded.

"Maybe there's too much going on, Cassie. Too much in your head, filling it up."

"Mostly Mama and the terrible baby," I said. "I do not plan to like that baby."

Grandfather sat down next to me.

"Remember when I first came here? You didn't much like me."

I thought Grandfather was mean then. I thought he was hateful and cranky.

"You changed," I said.

"You changed, too," said Grandfather.

"You changed more," I said, making Grandfather laugh.

I thought about what he said. I was different now. So was he. And Mama would be different soon.

Everything would be different. And it would never change back again. But I wrote it that way.

"Where is Beatrice?" I ask Mama.

"Gone," says Mama. "Gone away. Flown up to the sky with the doves."

All we have to take care of are our

goslings, Willie Jo and Margaret Louise and Madeleine.

Happily ever after. Just the way it always was.

8

Days went by, one by one by one, faster and faster. The haying would begin today. There were already neighbors and their horses and cutters out in the fields. The side yard was filled with tables for lunch later on.

I watched Mama all the time now, peeking at her from around doors and watching her nap in the afternoon. I watched her from the tree as the goslings followed her. At night I could hear her as she walked around the kitchen, and I'd tiptoe down the stairs and watch her until she went back to bed. I couldn't stop watching her.

I am Mama's protector. I will keep her
safe. I will save her from the terrible baby.
I have to watch.

"Cassie? What are you doing?"

I jumped as Grandfather came up behind me.

"I'm watching Mama."

"I can see that. You do it all the time. Why?"

"I have to!" I blurted it out.

Grandfather stared at me for a minute. Then he took my hand.

"Come with me," he said.

I looked back at Mama.

"I can't," I repeated.

"Come," repeated Grandfather, ignoring me.

He pulled me into the cool, dark barn. Caleb looked up from cleaning a bridle.

"Caleb. Your papa needs the bridles," said Grandfather.

"Now?"

"Yes."

Caleb picked up another bridle and went out to the field to hitch up the horses. He didn't look at me.

Grandfather pointed to a wooden trunk.

"Sit there, Cassie."

"I don't have time, Grandfather."

"Yes, you do."

"You are *still* mean," I told Grandfather.

Grandfather didn't answer. He sat down next to me.

"Caleb told me what you asked him in the middle of the night."

"Caleb shouldn't have done that," I said. "He was asleep, too. He didn't even remember what I said."

"Yes, he did," said Grandfather. "He did, Cassie," he repeated softly.

Grandfather took my hand again. I tried to pull it away, but he held on tightly.

"Cassie. You don't have to be afraid," he said. "Caleb's mama died when he was born because she was frail."

Frail. I knew that word. We had a lamb born once that was frail, and we'd brought it into the house to keep it warm, and we'd fed it from a bottle night and day. But the lamb had lived.

"Sarah is strong, Cassie."

His hand was warm, and I could feel tears fill my eyes.

"I am afraid," I whispered. "I have to keep Mama safe."

"No, Cassie. That isn't your job. That is your mama's job, and your papa's job. And mine."

I stared straight ahead, hoping the tears would not fall down my face. Grandfather held my hand, and the voices of Matthew and Caleb and Papa came closer. Finally, just before everyone came into the barn,

Grandfather leaned over and kissed me.

It was the kiss that made me cry. I ran away from Grandfather, past Matthew and Papa and Caleb, past Maggie and Violet's sister Rose and Violet in the yard. I ran past Mama, who turned to watch me. She called my name, but I ran into the house and up the stairs and into my room.

"Cassie!"

It was Mama's voice at the bottom of the stairs. I opened the door.

"Cassie, I want to speak with you."

I didn't answer.

"I'll climb up these stairs, Cassie."

"No. I'll come down," I said quickly.

Very slowly I walked down the stairs.

"Cassie. I know some things," said Mama.

"What things?"

"I know you watch me all the time," said Mama.

I started to shake my head, but Mama stopped me.

"I saw you in the night, watching. I saw you watching me with the goslings. I know you're afraid."

"Grandfather told you," I whispered.

"He didn't have to tell me," Mama said. "I'm smart, you know."

She smiled.

"I am fine, Cassie. I am strong."

"But you're old," I said.

"*Older*," corrected Mama.

Mama sat down at the kitchen table.

"I'll make a bargain with you, Cassie," she said. "You don't have to follow me everywhere anymore. You don't have to hide behind doors."

Mama had seen that, too?

"You don't have to get up in the night and watch me, because I will let you know if I need you."

"What do you mean?"

"I'll call you if I need something. I will call you when I'm going to have the baby."

I sat down next to Mama.

"You will? You will do that?"

Mama nodded.

"I promise," she said. "I promise, Cassie. You will be the first to know."

I leaned back in the chair. All of a sudden I was tired.

Mama stood up.

"I have to go help Maggie now," she said. "Why don't you go upstairs and sleep. You look tired."

"Will you . . . ?"

"Call you if I need you? Yes," said Mama.

Mama put her arms around me. That terrible baby was big inside her. It came between us so I couldn't put my arms all the way around her.

I went upstairs and lay down on my bed. I closed my eyes. There were no thoughts in my head. There were no words there. No stories. And when I slept there were no dreams.

9

We ate lunch in the shade of the house, all the workers and friends. The horses, near the barn, drank water out of buckets. Caleb washed them down to cool them. The air smelled the sharp, strong smell of cut hay. Little bits of hay hung in the still air.

Caleb sat next to Violet and they laughed at their own private words.

Still they laugh, the princess and Caleb. They laugh so much that laughter flies out of their mouths, goes up and away on the wind. When the wind dies, the laughter will float back to earth and make some sad, serious, surprised person laugh, too.

Rose drew a picture of Caleb and Violet, their faces pointed up, mouths open, looking like howling dogs. This made me laugh.

It felt strange to laugh. I hadn't laughed in a long time, and Mama looked over at me and smiled. Papa smiled, too, and Maggie brought out a tall, white, frosted cake with strawberries. Grandfather ate a bite, then two, then three.

"This is stupendous, Maggie," he said. "Exquisite!"

He caught me looking at him.

"You and Caleb taught me about words."

I nodded. Grandfather couldn't read when he had come back to the farm. All the years of his life he couldn't read. Until Caleb taught him.

"This cake is magnificent," said Grandfather. "Tasty, lovely, glorious, stunning! Could I have another piece?"

"Don't forget we have more haying to do," said Matthew.

"This cake can only help," said Grandfather.

Talk and words, some of them Grandfather's words, swirled around us until it was time for haying again.

We cleared the table, Lottie and Nick hoping for snacks.

"I'm going to town tomorrow," said Papa, carrying plates to the house. "Who needs something wonderful?"

Papa looked at me.

"Want to come, Cassie? Buy something perfect?"

Mama smiled.

"I'll have a new horse, if you don't mind," said Matthew.

"You could get me a buggy," said Maggie. "With a leather top."

"I'll have another piece of cake," said Grandfather, making everyone laugh.

"I'll come to town with you," said Caleb.

"I'm staying here. I know that," said Mama. "My back hurts today."

"I'll stay here, too," I said.

Mama took my hand.

"You go if you want, Cassie. Remember what I said."

I shook my head.

"No, I want to stay and write. I have many things to write."

"I'll bring you something. A present," called Caleb as he ran to bring in the horses. Grandfather walked out into the field, too.

The sky was so blue with a few clouds tossed above the land. Way off the cows moved slowly. A handful of sheep drank from the stream. A perfect day.

Perfect.

"I remember when you first came here, Sarah," said Maggie.

I listened carefully.

"You brought me flowers," said Mama. She imitated Maggie's soft Southern voice. "You said, 'you should have a garden wherever you are.'"

"What was Mama like then?" I asked.

Maggie grinned.

"She was strong-minded and opinionated."

"And she still is," I said.

Maggie and Mama laughed.

"Mama cried once because she missed you," I said.

"Oh I cried, too," said Maggie. Then she smiled. "But I'm back!"

I looked out and saw Grandfather coming in from the west meadow carrying something, a sheep following him, Caleb and Papa behind.

I ran out to the fence.

"Here's a present for you, Cassie,"
Grandfather said.

It was a new lamb. Very carefully
Grandfather put it down and it stood on
wobbly legs.

I grinned.

"It is Beatrice!" I said happily, leaning
down to pet the lamb.

I looked at Grandfather and Mama and
Papa. "Beatrice!"

---

*The clouds float above, slowly, slowly, like in a
dream. The air is sweet with hay.*

Beatrice has been born.

10

Mama handed Caleb a list.

"I'll stop at Anna's for a bit," Papa told her. "I'll be home late afternoon."

"I have Cassie here," Mama said.

"And they both have me," said Grandfather.

"Be sure to check that lamb," said Papa.

"Beatrice," I corrected Papa.

"Beatrice," said Papa with a smile. "I'm not sure her mother knows what to do with her."

The wagon started off, then stopped suddenly. Papa climbed down and came over and gave Mama a kiss.

"I forgot," he said. "I'll do that again when I get back."

"All this kissing," complained Grandfather.

"You should see Princess Violet and Caleb," I said.

"Cassie," warned Caleb.

The wagon clattered off and turned out the gate and went down the road, sending up little puffs of dust.

We walked over to the paddock fence. Beatrice stared at us with her little black eyes. She walked a little, then stopped and looked at us again.

"Beatrice," said Grandfather softly. "Don't really see how Beatrice can have a name when her mother doesn't have one."

"I think her name is Beatrice's Mother," said Mama.

"What kind of a name is that?" asked Grandfather.

"It's what we've got," said Mama with a smile.

Mama went off to the garden, followed by the goslings. Grandfather and I shoveled out stalls and laid down new hay for the horses. When we were done, I took my journal and sat in the meadow with Beatrice and Beatrice's Mother.

***

Beatrice is beautiful and wise and will grow up to be an intelligent and imaginative sheep.

Beatrice's Mother is not smart.

***

When Mama brought us sandwiches and fruit for lunch, I read them this. Grandfather nodded.

"I'm not sure sheep are known for their good sense," he said.

"Beatrice is unusual," I said.

The goslings saw Mama and ran over.

"Madeleine, I believe you're going to be

the largest of the three of you," said Mama. "And you, Margaret Louise, will always be the runt."

"Small and lovely, you mean," said Grandfather.

They bustled around Mama until, laughing, she shooed them away.

"You know," said Mama, "I'm going to go inside and rest. I feel tired."

"I'll come in, too," I said.

"I'll be in the barn," said Grandfather. "I'll come in later for a piece of cake."

"Cakes don't last forever," said Mama.

"Not with Grandfather around," I said.

Inside, Mama sat at the table while I poured tea. I took out my journal.

"Did you write in a journal when you were little?" I asked Mama.

Mama smiled.

"No, I never thought of it. You're lucky, Cassie. That journal is like an old friend, isn't it?"

"Sometimes."

There was a silence.

"Sometimes I write things in here that are nasty," I said.

"That's what a journal is for," said Mama. "To put down feelings. That way they don't clutter up your head."

I waited for a time while Mama drank tea.

"You know, I wrote something about you in here. And Beatrice."

"You did? Is that how you seemed to know her name?"

I nodded.

"I wrote that you did not have the terrible baby. You had a baby lamb named Beatrice."

Mama began to laugh. She laughed so hard that I began to laugh, too.

Finally she stopped to catch her breath.

"You know, it may be a good deal easier to raise that lamb than a terrible baby," she said.

Those words, "terrible baby," sounded funny in Mama's voice. It seemed to give me some courage.

"And I wrote that you made Caleb take care of it because all it did was sleep and bleat. You said I was more beautiful than Beatrice. And smarter."

My voice got smaller.

"And you loved me best."

Mama did not laugh. She reached over and touched my cheek.

"And I do love you the best of all the eight-year-olds in this very house," she said. "And I have enough room in me, Cassie. If I can love three troublesome goslings, I will share some love with the terrible baby."

I smiled. I loved it when Mama said "terrible baby." It was as if she had come over to my side. We would both have to deal with the terrible baby when it came.

"Oh no," cried Mama. "Help me, Cassie! That terrible baby is rude and

*ugly and smelly and as dumb as a stick.
And it cannot read or write. Take it away.
Take it far, far away and come back and
read to me."*

"Cass."

Mama's voice was faint. I stopped writing.
"Yes?"

"Remember when I said I'd let you know
when I needed you?"

I nodded.

"Well, I need you now," said Mama. "I
think it is time."

I almost asked time for what, and then I
saw Mama's face. It was pale and tight.

"Go get Maggie," said Mama. "I'm going
to the bedroom to lie down, Cassie. The
baby is coming."

I stood up, my journal falling off the
table. I left it where it fell.

"Someone has to ride over to get her. Her phone doesn't work," said Mama. "I think you'd better hurry."

Mama stood up and held on to the chair. She didn't look like Mama all of a sudden. She looked like someone far away from me.

"I'll get Grandfather," I said.

I ran out the door and across the yard to the barn.

"Grandfather! Grandfather!" I screamed.

Grandfather came out of the barn.

"Mama says it's time. The baby is coming!" I said. I could hardly catch my breath. "We have to get Maggie."

Grandfather ran into the barn to get a horse.

"Go in with your mama. We'll be back."

He galloped off, out the gate, down the road to Maggie's house.

I took a deep breath and ran into the bedroom to sit with Mama.

"Read me the part again about the cows floating through the barn," said Mama, lying on the bed.

I read her most of my journal, even the mean parts, as we waited for Maggie. But Mama didn't mind. She smiled sometimes. Sometimes she laughed out loud. Sometimes she pressed her lips together and didn't say anything, and I knew she hurt.

After a long time I heard noises outside. I ran to the front door and opened it. Maggie and Grandfather were there, Maggie getting off the dappled horse.

"How is she?" called Maggie.

"I've been reading to her. Sometimes she laughs," I said.

Maggie smiled and kissed me on the cheek.

"That's wonderful," she said. "I'll go take care of her."

She went past me, and when she did I

felt suddenly safe again.

Grandfather sat heavily on a porch chair.

"It has been years since I galloped on a horse," he said.

"You looked like a hero," I whispered.

"Well then, I need a piece of cake," he said.

He looked at me and then got up and put his arms around me.

We stood that way on the porch for a long, long time.

———•———

My journal lay on the floor, untouched. Grandfather ate cake. We didn't talk. I called Anna on the phone, but no one answered. I washed the dishes, then saw that I'd already washed them. I swept the floor and peeled carrots and potatoes to put in a pot of hot water for soup. It wasn't until the goslings pecked at the door that I burst into tears. I went out to the porch, but it wasn't me they were looking for. It was Mama.

"When's Jacob coming home?" asked Grandfather.

"I don't know," I said.

Hurry, hurry, Papa.

"Maybe I'll go to the barn and do some work," said Grandfather.

I heard Mama cry out, and then Maggie's soft voice.

"No, please," I said to Grandfather. "Stay with me."

Grandfather held my hand and we watched the road for a dust cloud that would mean that Papa was coming home. It seemed like hours went by. But the wagon didn't come. And didn't come.

And then, later, when I was almost asleep, my head on Grandfather's shoulder, it was Maggie who came out to the porch, smiling, to tell us that the baby was here.

"Already?" Grandfather was astonished.

"Yes," said Maggie. "Cassie, Sarah wants to see you."

"Me?"

Maggie nodded.

"Go on, go on."

"Mama's all right?"

"Your mama is fine," said Maggie.

I stopped at Mama's door. That baby was inside. I didn't want to see it. I didn't want to know it. I pushed the door open and saw Mama, lying in bed, her eyes closed. Next to her was a wrapped bundle. Mama turned her head and smiled at me.

"Thank you for reading to me, Cassie. You did a fine job."

I stood still.

"Come on," said Mama. "Come in and see the terrible baby."

I looked at Mama, shocked. I moved closer. Mama patted the bed for me to sit, so I did.

And then she picked up the bundle and gave it to me.

I sat there, staring at Mama. After a moment I looked down. My heart beat faster. The baby had a round head and no hair. The baby had dark, dark eyes that looked up at me, a little like Beatrice's eyes. The baby yawned then, making the smallest sound. I looked at the tiny fingers, with tiny nails. I bent down, remembering what Papa had said about how I smelled when I was a baby. Papa knew.

"This is supposed to be Beatrice," I whispered.

Mama smiled.

"That may be," she whispered back to me, "but that is a strange name for a boy."

A boy.

"I don't have any words," I said to Mama.

"I know," she said. "But you will."

All of a sudden I heard noises in the kitchen, Papa's voice, and Caleb's. Laughter from Grandfather. Then Papa stood at the door, looking pale and scared, Caleb behind him. And Grandfather.

"I brought you a perfect gift, Cassie!" Caleb blurted out.

"No," I said, my voice soft. "The perfect gift is here."

I looked up at Papa.

"He is a terrible baby."

I smiled at Mama.

"But he's more perfect than the moon."

PATRICIA MacLACHLAN

is the author of many beloved novels for young readers, including ARTHUR, FOR THE VERY FIRST TIME, winner of the Golden Kite Award for fiction; THE FACTS AND FICTIONS OF MINNA PRATT; and SARAH, PLAIN AND TALL, winner of the Newbery Medal, as well as its sequels, SKYLARK and CALEB'S STORY. She is the author of several picture books, including THREE NAMES and ALL THE PLACES TO LOVE. She also coauthored PAINTING THE WIND and BITTLE with her daughter, Emily.